# This book belongs to:

Rosie Beck
&
SENNEN

For Emily and Robin M.B.
For Leo N.S.

First published in 2014 by
Hodder Children's Books
This edition published in 2018

Hodder Children's Books
An imprint of Hachette Children's Group
Part of Hodder & Stoughton
Carmelite House, 50 Victoria Embankment
London EC4Y 0DZ

A catalogue record of this book is available
from the British Library.

ISBN: 978 1 444 94716 8
10 9 8 7 6 5 4 3

Printed in China

An Hachette UK Company

www.hachette.co.uk

# Best Friends

Mara Bergman　　Nicola Slater

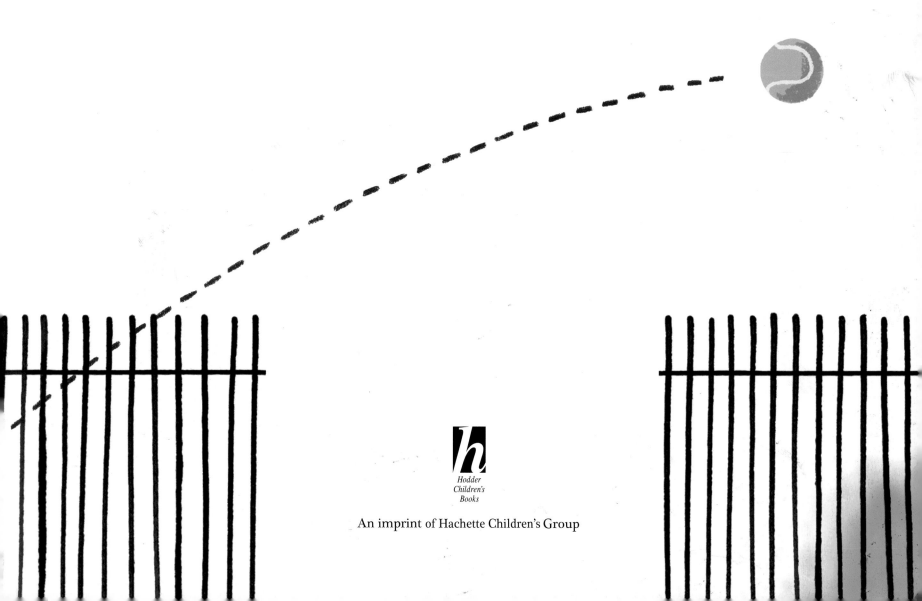

Hodder
Children's
Books

An imprint of Hachette Children's Group

D exter McFadden McSimmons McClean,
the dog with the longest legs anyone's seen,
was chasing a ball as fast as he could,
over the bridge and into the wood.

*Meanwhile…*

Daisy the dachshund was strolling along, humming and whistling to her favourite song.

She ignored the dark

*FLASH*

as it shot through the wood

and followed her ball just as fast as she could.

*Meanwhile...*

Lily had been for a wash and a cut
when she went to the park for a walk and a strut.

She too was chasing
her favourite ball,
ignoring the other dogs,
**big** ones and small.

Three dogs
were running.
Where would
they go?

and **Daisy**
**SO** slow,

**Dexter** like lightning

and **Lily**, who hated to dirty her claws,

ran ever so lightly
on tippy-toe paws.

*Meanwhile...*

William was running
as fast as he could,
calling for Dexter,
who ran through
the wood,

*while…*

Jack was happily
strolling along,
looking for Daisy
and singing a song,

and…

Maddie was searching
and searching for Lily,
who'd just had her hair cut
and looked rather silly!

*"Dexter!"*
called William,

then Jack,
*"Daisy, here!"*

Maddie
called, *"Lily!"*

But did they appear?

The Millers were having a picnic that day

and **jumped up**
as Dexter
came charging their way,

and **Daisy** gave someone
a terrible

fright...

while **Lily** got mixed up
with somebody's kite.

Sandwiches, newspapers, blankets went flying,

and one little baby kept
crying and **crying!**

But soon they were off again,
dashing about, ignoring each call,
every cry, every shout.

"*Dexter!*" called William,

then Jack, "*Daisy, here!*"

Maddie called, "*Lily!*"

But did they appear?

THEN...

the children grew worried. What was that sound?
They ran to the stream...

SPLISH!

SPLASH!

...and look what they found:

**Dexter** and **Daisy**
and **Lily** all wet!

Each was the soggiest, happiest pet.
With a **wriggle** and **shake,** the dogs made a splatter.
The children got soaked, but it didn't matter!

And this is the way that our story ends –
the children and dogs became…

# best friends!

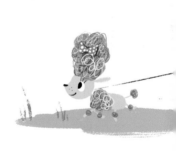

# Look out for these other great picture books, perfect to share with children:

## SNIP SNAP, ALLIGATOR!
Mara Bergman and Nick Maland

## SNIP SNAP, LOOK WHO'S BACK!
Mara Bergman and Nick Maland

## Six Dinner Sid
INGA MOORE

## OI FROG!
KES GRAY & JIM FIELD

## WANTED: The Perfect Pet
'A hoot.' THE SUNDAY TIMES
Fiona Roberton

For fun activities, further information and to order, visit www.hodderchildrens.co.uk